LIFE BEFORE DAMAGED VOL. 5
THE FERRO FAMILY

BY:

H.M. WARD

HWM PRESS

www.SexyAwesomeBooks.com

COPYRIGHT

H.M. WARD PRESS
First Edition: February 2015
ISBN: 9781630350604

LIFE BEFORE DAMAGED VOL. 5

SEE YOU LATER, ALLIGATOR!

August 10th, 12:03am

Before I know what's going on, Pete grabs me by the wrist and pulls me from the dance floor. "Grab your things, we're leaving." He glances back at me and those deep blue eyes rake over my body. His voice drops and becomes a forced whisper, "Now."

I'm stunned for a moment. This is happening? This is really happening! Ah! I am so going to have filthy hot sex tonight. My only regret? Being too drunk to fully commit every detail to memory. I'm not naïve. By this time tomorrow, I'll be yesterday's news and he'll move on to some other woman, but for tonight, he's mine and I'm going to make every second count. Hopefully, Erin is right and after this tryst I'll move forward and put this crazy infatuation behind me. Because this is just a lusty dream. There's nothing more, not with Pete Ferro. I'd be insane to fall in love with him, I mean look at this—he's jerking me off the dance floor, practically growling. I'm finally the booby blonde. I let out a little eeep. My hands slap to my mouth to cover the sound.

Pete's badass face breaks into a crooked grin. "What was that?"

I shake my head and shrug my shoulders, letting my hands fall to my sides. My face is burning bright red, so I lower my gaze to the floor. Pete takes my chin in his hand and tilts my head up. Our gazes meet and he leans in close before breathing in my ear, "Get your coat."

Don't giggle. Don't giggle. My mouth twitches, but I manage to keep the hysterical glee in my stomach. I don't mean to, but as I attempt a sexy, hip-swaying saunter away from him, it turns into something else. Three steps further and I'm skipping. I pretty much slam into the bar to stop, grabbing my bag and coat. My elegant move catches Ricky's attention.

Placing my palms on the bar, I hoist myself up and lean over the wood to give Ricky a quick kiss on the cheek. "See you later, alligator!" I drop down and feel a rush of air swish my skirt up a little bit. It makes me want to dance more but when I turn around and see Pete, I remember what I'm doing.

When Ricky glances up to see who I'm leaving with, he frowns. "I don't like this, doll. That cat is bad news. You got your phone with you?" Ricky wipes the bar with a damp cloth, removing sticky traces of alcohol and fruit juice. If he rubs any harder, he'll strip the thick varnish off.

Yanking on my coat, I shrug off his disapproving look and pull the hood over my head. Ricky is being a silly old worry wart. He's leaning against the bar, just within reach, giving me a super sourpuss. I give his cheek a reassuring pat, but Ricky cringes and I pull my hand back. I might have touched him a bit too hard. You shouldn't hear a slapping sound when patting someone. I'm suddenly laughing again. "Sorry! I didn't mean to bitchslap you." I point to my tiny guns and push on the muscle, trying to beef it up, "They don't look like much, but once in a while I underestimate their strength." When his mood remains static, I frown at him. "I'll be fine and yes, I have my phone. Why?" I don't plan on turning my phone on. Too many bad feelings and I don't want to listen to voicemails. Right now, I want to feel good and I know Pete can do that for me.

"You call me if you need me, okay?" Ricky tosses the rag over his shoulder and it lands perfectly in a little bucket on the floor behind him. How does he do that? I swear the guy has the most amazing coordination I've ever seen.

"I will."

Before I can turn around, there's a familiar hand on my shoulder. Pete's deep voice follows. "Is there a problem?"

Ricky glares at him, jaw tight, but locked shut. Normally he'd say no and smile, but Ricky's normal carefree attitude is gone. If they were girls, they'd be pulling hair and clawing each other right now.

"There's no problem as long as you don't hurt my girl. If you do, you'll deal with me."

Pete laughs. It's one harsh breath. His hand tightens on my shoulder as he looks Ricky over. "Your girl is leaving with me, so that would make her my girl. Back off. If you don't, I'll make you."

"Hey," I put a hand on Pete's chest to calm him down and push him back. When did he get so close to the bar? But I can't make him budge. The man is a moose. I giggle as the thought of moving a moose crosses my mind. I can see four legs up in the air and the thing tied to my back with rope as I walk hunched over like an aerodynamic ninety-year-old.

Ricky's attitude clicks up a level. "She's not your girl. She's wasted and only assholes and losers take a girl home when she's drunk. Since I know you're both, I think you should leave her here and walk away." While Ricky talks, he pushes a finger against Pete's chest.

Bad move. Not good. "Guys, stop! Ricky, I know him."

"So do I," Ricky bites back, not bothering to look at me.

Pete's shoulders square off and I feel the way his arms ripple like he wants to rip Ricky's head off. "I'm not leaving her here so you can finally get her alone."

"I've been alone with her, dickwad. You have no idea what the fuck you're—"

I laugh and cut Ricky off. "Not like that! Stop messing with him, Ricky. You know Pete likes to punch pretty faces and it'd be a shame to do damage to yours. Pete, I'm all yours. Let's go." I fasten my coat as I speak. When I look up, I catch Pete and Ricky staring at each other with that guy stare like they're throwing punches with their eyeballs.

Placing a hand on Pete's arm, I lean in close to his ear and whisper, "I'd rather you spent the night touching me than punching him. Let's go."

That ends it. Pete escorts me to the parking lot and I see that he's brought his car, not his motorcycle. He fishes his keys from out of his pockets and opens my door. I duck into my seat and after he closes the door and gets into his side, he looks at me, raising an eyebrow. "Is there a problem?"

My disappointment is obviously plastered across my face. I guess the protruding bottom lip, stuck out in an exaggerated pout will do that. "No. No problem. I was kind of hoping to take a ride on your bike tonight. That's all." I shrug.

Pete looks through the windshield and says with a questioning grin, "It's raining," as if I am a moron, too stupid to notice the weather.

"And? I've seen you ride that thing, mister!" I'm all pointy fingers as I talk. "You don't look like the kind of person who'll stop himself from doing something dangerous like riding a bike in torrential rain."

"True. But I'm not going to bring a woman back on my bike when it's raining, and leaving alone is never an option." He gives me a wink.

REGINA OR JENNY?

August 10th, 12:31 am

Oh. My stomach drops into my shoes and I try to hide it by looking out the window, my mind wandering back to unpleasant thoughts. They vanish quickly, though, when he starts the car and backs up so fast that he leaves half his tires on the pavement. Pete shifts gears and we take off at spaceship speed, not slowing down to accommodate surrounding motorists. Pete cuts everyone off, weaving his way through whatever traffic gets in his way. I hold my breath and reach for the leather oh-shit-strap, wanting to hold on for dear life.

"Don't," Pete growls without looking at me. My hand is half way to the strap.

"Sorry, I don't want to die before I get laid." Did I just say that out loud? I'm about to crawl under the seat when Pete cuts across the lane into oncoming traffic to pass another car. Fuck it! I grab the strap and hang on as we swerve back into our lane.

Next time I look over at Pete, there's a lazy smile on his face. "I can't believe you said that."

"Neither can I. But let's face it, that would suck."

Pete laughs and loosens his death grip on the wheel. We sit in silence and when Pete hits the highway, I finally release the strap and sink back into my seat. Fondling my phone, I wonder what Anthony's doing at the moment. Did he love me at all?

Did he kick Kitty out when he realized I'd caught him? Is he still trying to reach me? Has he called my parents yet? How long has he been cheating on me? The questions just keep coming and I want them to shut up. I'm past the point of crying. In fact, I feel empty inside. Like someone took a chunk of my life and just tossed it out the window like trash. Anthony will never propose, he'll never become my husband, we'll never have those kids I'd imagined.

My future is a blank canvas and it's not an entirely bad feeling. In fact, it feels surprisingly good. I can be whoever I want to be from now on and right now, I want so badly to be the object of someone's desire. It'll override the complete rejection lingering inside of me. If I were different, if I were prettier, he wouldn't have cheated.

I'm surprised when my door opens and Pete extends a hand, to help me out of the car. Once upright, I wobble on my heels a bit and it takes a while to register we're back at the Ferro mansion.

My jaw drops. "This is your house." So not a good sign. Pete Ferro doesn't take women back to his house for booty calls. He told me that himself. Why would he bring me here then? The only reason that comes to mind is that he has no real intention of sleeping with me, after all. This is not his slut palace.

"Yeah, I kind of realized that." Pete's tone is unreadable. I can't tell why he took me here. I thought he wanted me. My heart drops into my shoes as I realize he was just trying to save me from the frat boys.

"Maybe I wanted to be Jenny."

"What?" Pete glances sideways at me and takes my hand, tugging me toward the door.

I yank my hand free. "I mean it. How do you know what I want? Don't make assumptions. You're not my mother and if I want to nail a frat boy, leave me to it!"

Pete looks back and forth. There's a servant standing nearby, no smile on his face, still as stone. Pete sighs and talks slowly, "Does Jenny want a frat boy? Or a Ferro? Because no matter how sloshed you are there's no way in hell you're getting both."

My fear falls away. "You want me?"

"Not in the driveway, but it's worth your while to come inside and find out." Pete is being sweet. I doubt he'd put up with this from one of his booby blondes. They're all sugar and would have been ear-fucking him all the way out here. I was staring out the window wondering why my boyfriend cheated on me. My mind wasn't on Pete at all.

I nod and take his hand.

As we head to the door, the servant that's been watching my hissy fit moves forward to take the car off to the garage. Pete helps me up the few steps to the front door and motions for me to be quiet. He leads us down the now slightly familiar hallways, towards his wing of the house and opens a door into a room I haven't seen yet. Based on smell alone, I know it's his bedroom.

Maybe he is breaking his rules, after all.

"Stop worrying." His words make me realize I've been holding my breath. "Look around, jump on the bed, and make yourself at home."

"Does that mean strip? Because sometimes a guy says make yourself comfy and he means take your clothes off. What do you mean? Because I'm super confused right now and—"

"Jenny."

"Yes."

"Stop talking." I nod and shut my mouth. That's when I finally look around. There's a bed. A king sized bed with thick wooden posters that spiral up into the air. I shiver looking at it. My mind starts going wild, imagining all the things he could do, will do, to me in that bed. Pete closes the door behind us and steps forward to help me out of my wet coat.

"So what is this? Are you breaking your rules again, Ferro?"

"You have no idea, Granz. I'll go hang this up for you." He takes the raincoat and disappears in the ensuite bathroom.

Ok, Gina. Are we doing comfy or comfy? I stop thinking because I can't stop staring at his bed. It's huge and fluffy. The mattress is calling to me, saying jump on me, Gina. I can't resist. I run at it and jump, falling from the air and hitting the bed spread-eagle, face down. I giggle like a lunatic and hug a pillow before I flip over. I sigh and notice Pete leaning against the bedpost, his arms folded over his chest. He laughs softly.

"Going for the subtle spread-eagle or was that seriously a face-plant into my pillows?" He grins, revealing his dimple, and a strand of dark hair falls across his face.

"Wouldn't you like to know?" Pushing off his bed, I start to walk toward him, making sure I sway my hips. I'm smooth for all of two seconds before one of my heels gets caught in the plush rug on the floor and I stumble. Luckily for me, Pete is quick and catches me before I end up face first on the floor, making a bigger ass of myself than I already have.

"Feeling suicidal tonight? Weren't you dancing in those?" He holds me tighter and smirks, making me want to lick that dimple right off his face. I didn't think I had a thing for dimples. Pete is watching me closely. "So is this Gina or Jenny? Did you escape from somewhere? Is there an ax in your purse that I should be afraid of?"

I giggle and snort laugh and it's not seductive at all. "I wish I could break free." My voice is hollow and flat. Even while drunk, that subject is a sore spot.

Seeming to realize his mistake, Pete cups my face with his warm hands and tips my head back. "You're free with me. I won't force you to be someone you're not and I suspect the real you is more Jenny than anyone realizes."

I smile at him, uncertain. "No one knows what it feels like, how suffocating it can be. Then things happened and I'm sick of waiting for the right moment, you know? What if it never comes? Or what if it came and went and I was too dense to see it? I can't be Regina Granz forever." I shiver as the corners of my mouth turn down. The thought makes me sick.

His soft, sweet voice falls upon me like a caress. "I know what you mean, every bit of it. Every failed expectation is a noose. Every social outing is a witch hunt and I feel lucky if I can manage to sneak away." His timing is as perfect as his words.

"And find a fireplace mantel?" Pete's cheeks flush as his eyes dip to my neckline. "Oh my God, is the great sexy man beast blushing?"

"I don't blush, I just get hot and bothered. Like right now, with you—I'm very hot and very bothered."

The butterflies in my stomach wake up with those words. His arms around me are freeing, a heavenly escape from reality. I look up and give him a shy smile and spread my hands across the front of his shirt. Going up on my tiptoes and leaning in closer toward his ear, I whisper, with what I am hoping is a seductive voice, "What are you planning on doing about it, Ferro? Should we jump on the bed?"

"Only if you're under me."

"I see." I purposefully exhale the words

towards his ear. It takes all the courage I have to drop a small kiss on his neck, followed by a tiny bite. It's really just dragging my teeth along the skin as I close my jaw, not painful at all. I feel his hands tighten around my arms and his head dip towards my neck.

His lips brush the skin, but he doesn't do anything. He just stays there. This is progress, but I need to up the stakes a bit more.

I push him back a step. The look on his face is ecstasy and agony wrapped into a sexy body that's wound too tight. He's going to snap and when he does, I can't wait. The thought leaves me breathless. The hungry kisses and passionate touches I imagined will be nothing compared to what he's about to do. I can sense it.

His lips are slightly parted and his tongue darts out to moisten them. His eyes have taken on a lustful darkness and his chest is rising and falling more rapidly than it was just seconds ago. A rush of excitement goes through me as I realize I really can have this kind of effect on a man. And not just any man, but Pete. I refuse to give Kitty another thought. Anthony is gone.

I take a couple steps back until the backs of my knees bump into the bed behind me. The rain is pounding on the window panes. There's an occasional burst of light, followed by increasingly loud thunder, making the atmosphere even more electric.

Pete looks away, breaking the connection. My stomach goes into freefall when he says my name.

"Gina, I…" No, that's the sound of regret and it's creeping back into his voice. Pete takes a step forward as if he wants to say more, but I put up a finger, silently asking him to stay where he is.

"You said be me, but I'm nervous." The butterflies are now threatening to fly up and escape through my mouth and I'm praying that they stay put. Now is not the time to be a sick drunk. What if he doesn't like what he sees? Is that why he's backing off? I'm not begging, but this version of me wouldn't let him leave either. "Don't make it hard on me, Pete."

I don't give him a chance to respond. With the knot undone at the waist of my dress, it's easy to push the fabric off my shoulders. The slinky fabric falls slowly from my arms, exposing my corset. Pete stands there silently watching.

I wiggle my hips and shimmy out of the dress, letting the fabric slide down my body and pool at my feet. One foot at a time, I step out of my dress and push it aside with my toe. My heel snags on the fabric and it gets stuck like a piece of toilet paper on a wet shoe. I smile nervously and try to shake it off, but it doesn't let go. I look like an idiot in a corset. Pete watches me shake it once, then twice. On the third time, my arms are drifting up to cover my corset.

That's when he drops to one knee and pulls the dress away from my foot. He stays there, bending on one knee like a knight. My heart pounds faster and I can't believe he's doing this. His cheek is so close to my leg I can feel its warmth, and when he gently sets my foot down, he kisses the side of my ankle. A jolt of lust races through me and I feel like I'm going to fall. My knees weaken and I make a small sound without meaning to.

When he stands again, his eyes are level with mine. "Continue." It's one word, one perfect word.

Shivering, I lift one foot, placing it on

his bed. Reaching down slowly, I unfasten the garters one at a time. I wonder how I compare to what he's used to, but I'm not sure if I really care anymore. Pete is watching me. He's here with me. After both thigh highs are removed and tossed aside, Pete's eyes scan my body from bottom to top, taking in my pink satin and black lace outfit. After wearing the tight corset for hours the boning pokes painfully into my skin, but I'd take the pain any day to look like this in front of the man I've been fantasizing about for weeks. It makes me feel like the confident, sensual, sexual woman I want him to see me as and not the meek, mousy Regina Granz he saved only a couple of weeks ago.

That girl doesn't exist anymore.

Pete eyes me, taking his time, drinking me in like he may never stop. Heart pounding hard, I feel like I may die. I'm trying to translate his body language, but he's sending such confusing messages. He's not saying or doing anything, just staring at me from under those dark lashes. His body shows his lust. The rapid breathing and the way his hands are clutching and releasing his shirt repetitively betray him. But his face.

His face is what concerns me because he looks conflicted. I wish I knew why.

He walks closer to me so slowly. The controlled movements, and the way he draws them out, are driving me insane. All I can think of is having his hands and lips and tongue all over me. To have him push me down onto the bed and make me feel things I can't even begin to imagine. Things I've only read about in books and seen in movies and dreamt of many times over. He's right there in front of me, but he's not closing the distance between us. Just when I think I'll scream for him to do something, he unfolds his arms, gently places his hands on my cheeks and brushes my cheekbones with his thumbs. It's a caress as soft as silk.

"You're so beautiful," he exhales. It's barely audible, but I hear it. Those words make my heart soar. He's called me beautiful before, but never like this. This time it's like an homage or adulation, it's like he's talking about someone sacred. No one has ever told me I'm beautiful in such a way, not ever.

He leans in and the tip of his nose brushes along the side of mine, our lips almost touching. I lift up my chin, to close the distance, but he backs away ever so slightly. He's holding back his kiss and I want to taste it so badly. There's a struggle going on in his eyes like he's deciding if he should do this or not. I wish I knew what to say or do to convince him.

I take a chance and say, "Kiss me, Peter, please?"

His eyes close and his lips finally come down on mine, gently. His hands move from my cheeks to my hair and he holds me in his kiss. His lips brush mine once, twice. His kiss is soft and tender, which knocks the wind out of me. I was expecting hard and passionate, but this is so much stronger. The tenderness makes my knees weak and as I feel his tongue stroke my lips I start to wobble. I open up to him and let him in. My hands tangle in his hair while his hands drift down along my shoulders, across my corset, his thumbs grazing the edge of my breasts and finally resting at my waist.

The kiss gets more passionate with each passing second. He's exploring every inch of my mouth with his sinful tongue and I do the same to him. We're stroking and tasting each other. I let out a little whimper and he squeezes my hips with his fingers before pulling me against him. I can feel how much he wants me through the layers of clothing, and it ignites a fire deep inside me.

There are too many layers between us. I want them gone. I want to feel my body brush up against his, skin to skin. As if reading my mind, his hands move to the back of my corset. Just when I think he's going to unfasten the hooks, he breaks the kiss and steps back.

We're both breathless, but his face looks pained, as if stepping away is causing him actual physical agony. Pete runs a hand over his face and exhales. "I can't, Gina."

He can't do this to me, not again. I'm determined to finish this. "No." With determination, I slowly, purposefully, unfasten the corset hooks, one by one. I need to get him to touch me. It's the only way. My heart is pounding so hard in my chest, I think I may die before the night is through.

By the time my hands reach the last hook, Pete steps closer and reaches behind me. He puts his hands on mine to stop me, but it's too late. I let the piece of lingerie fall to the ground, exposing my aching breasts to him. My nipples are so taut that they hurt. I want to feel his skin on mine so I reach for the hem of his shirt. He doesn't hesitate to help me take it off and toss it to the side, giving me hope.

My breath catches at the sight of him. He's perfect. All toned muscle and smooth skin. He is completely unmarred. Not a single tattoo to ruin the perfect beauty that is Pete Ferro. I run my hands along his chest, trailing the tips of my fingers down to his stomach, feeling every defined muscle.

I place a small kiss on his chest before I sit down on the bed and lean back. Reaching out, I hook my fingers in the waistband of his pants and pull him toward me. When I'm finally lying on my back, he climbs on top of me, propping himself up on one arm, while his other hand trails up and down my body.

When he reaches one of my breasts, he hesitates. His touch is feather light. His thumb brushes over my nipple once and I gasp, arching my back and clutching the comforter underneath me. I hold myself back from screaming out loud. That light touch gets me hot in places down below and I'm in serious danger of overheating too quickly.

Breathless, he starts to say, "Gina, we need to stop. I—"

I don't let him finish his sentence. I push myself up with my hands and meet his lips in a hard, passionate kiss. Our tongues dance together once more. He lowers us down onto the bed and I part my legs so he can settle himself between them. He presses himself against my core and lets out a low growl from deep in his throat. It resonates within me, making me even hotter. I wrap my legs around his hips and push against him once, needing to ease the ache.

Our lips part and his kisses trail along my jaw and down to my neck. My breathing increases, the anticipation is too much. I need him so badly it hurts. I feel his tongue swirl around my nipple and a hand slides down in between us, cupping me, over my panties putting pressure right where I need it the most. What I have to say next is one of the hardest things I've ever had to say but I need this. I have to tell him what I truly want and I'm scared. This goes against everything I am, everything I was.

Finally feeling brave enough, I say it.

"Make me forget everything. Please, fuck me hard so I can't remember."

His kisses stop and he removes his hand. I'm lost in a tidal wave of pleasure, waiting for him to give in. Pete pushes back up on his arms, face flushed, still breathing heavily. He looks at me confused, eyebrows pinched together.

With a gentle hand, he pushes my hair away from my face. "Remember what? What's the matter? Gina, tell me. What were you doing at the club tonight?" His voice is soft, cautious, just like it was that first night we met, when he saved me and was worried about my safety.

A lump forms in my throat. I don't want to remember. I just want to get lost in the feeling of him. "I just want to forget." I don't know why I say that to him but his eyes are searching mine and I can't lie—not to him.

Pete reaches over. I'm assuming he's retrieving a condom from his bedside table. It's when my mind registers the feeling of fabric sliding over my chest, that the thick cloud of lust dissipates from my head and the crushing sense of shame and mortification set in once more. He's putting a blanket over me.

He's not going to go through with it.

I watch as he pushes himself off of the bed, and walks over to pick up his shirt on the floor, and puts it back on. I don't know if I can muster the courage to get him back. Not after this. I've already exposed so much of myself, did things, said things. If that wasn't enough to entice him, maybe I really do suck at this whole sex thing.

I sit up on the bed and keep myself covered with the blanket, keeping it tucked under my arms and I stare down at my fingers, completely humiliated.

"Talk to me. What happened? What are you trying so hard to forget?" he asks, his voice is full of concern. It's not the arrogant, condescending tone I'm used to hearing from him. When I don't answer, he sits next to me on the bed and lifts my chin up with his finger, studying my face. I don't look into his eyes. Instead, I look at his shirt. His tight, black tee that hugs his toned chest so perfectly. That same chest that I was touching with my bare hands and bare breasts only moments ago.

"You didn't answer me before. Where's your boyfriend, Gina? Talk to me. What did he do to you?" A tear escapes my eye and rolls down my cheek. The longer I stay quiet, the angrier Pete gets, his fists balling up and his jaw clenching tight. I might as well tell him the truth before he gets the wrong impression and goes off on a rampage, giving Anthony free dental work.

"I caught him with another woman tonight. We're through." I still can't look him in the eye. The humiliation is too much. Now he knows just how much of a failure I really am, more than ever. I smirk, wanting to lash out. "It doesn't matter. It's the same old story twice in one night."

Pete lets out a rush of air and, from the corner of my eye, I see him angrily stomping away towards the door to his room. He's leaving again.

He jumps in surprise when a black stiletto shoe hits the door, only an inch from his face. He's even more surprised when the second shoe hits the same spot. "I didn't have to miss. Don't you dare walk out on me without an explanation. I pour my heart out to you and I get the back of your head. What the fuck is that?"

He rounds on me and he's in my face, all fury and rage, "What I do is my business!

And stop attacking me. You're acting like a lunatic, swaying whichever way your emotions blow."

I kneel on the bed so that we are eye to eye. "No one is getting blown tonight. As for the shoe to the head, you walked away. Again. Thanks for making me feel like I'm not good enough—not for you or anyone!" I'm yelling in his face and holding the blanket tightly against me because there is no way I'm ever letting him see me naked again.

He straightens and pulls at his hair with both hands in obvious frustration. "I'm not doing this," he yells back. He walks back toward the door to his room, grabs his black leather jacket and puts his hand on the doorknob to leave.

I shouldn't, but I can't help it. The words rush out between tears, "What's so wrong with me?"

He turns his head, looking over his shoulder with a pained expression. "Nothing's wrong with you. That's the problem."

The door closes behind him and I want to cry. I mumble into my hands, "Then why'd you leave me?"

UNDERCOVER JENNY

August 10th, 8:14am

Smoke.

Screaming.

Hands pulling at me, scorching my arms. I try to pull away, but I can't. I cry for help, but nobody hears me. Only the dead and the dying can hear me, but they can't save me. In fact, they're trying to bring me down with them. I'm going to burn. I'm going to die. Somebody help me, please!

I jump and realize it was only a dream. I feel like there's a vice around my head, squeezing my brains out through my ears. Not to mention the constant pounding in my head. It's like a ceaseless drumbeat with its loud thu-thump, thu-thump, thu-thump! I'm never drinking again! Fingers are gently stroking through my hair, combing through the tangles. The feeling is soothing but a little unnerving as I realize I'm supposed to be in bed alone. A soothing voice is lulling me back to sleep. I'll figure all of this out later as I'm pulled into a dreamless slumber.

Something shifts beside me and I'm pulled out of my sleep once more. I'm lying on my side, curled up in a ball with my head resting on a very firm, very warm pillow of... muscle? My body is cuddling into someone, our legs entwined, and that someone is awake because he--oh shit! I hope he's a he. Judging by muscle tone, the hair on his legs and the masculine, musky smell on his skin, he must be a he. He is still combing through my hair with his fingers. Am I in bed with some stranger? I can't be with Anthony, he cheated on me and he doesn't like to cuddle. The feeling of warmth and closeness is nice and I could easily stay like this all day but my foggy brain keeps trying to put the pieces together. I remember leaving Anthony's to go to the club, drinking insane amounts of rum with Ricky, dancing, and a... frat boy?

Panic starts to bubble up when I realize that I may have just hooked up with some random guy and possibly made one of the stupidest mistakes of my life. But then I remember something else.

Pete. He was there too. We went back to his place and I—

Oh.

My.

God.

The memories come rushing back as fast as that slinky sports' car of his. I stripped, very clumsily I might add, in front of him and asked him to fuck me... I'll never be able to look him in the face again. My best bet to live down this humiliation would be to move to another state.

At least I've solved the mystery of who the man lying next to me is. Maybe, if I pretend to sleep, he'll eventually get up and leave. The man has to get up eventually and when he does, I can sneak out. Yeah, that's it. I can be all super-secret agent and leave without anyone seeing me. Undercover Jenny. Dun-dun-dun.

"Good morning. How's the hangover?"
I feel his voice vibrate in his chest.

So much for my secret agent plan. He must have noticed a change in my breathing or felt my body stiffen or something. I blink a couple of times to chase off the sleep in my eyes. I'm treated to the sight of his flawless torso gently rising and falling with his every breath and I'm suddenly very aware that I have my head resting on it, as well as a hand. I need to stop touching him, now, but he feels so comfortable. I feel like I'm on a diet and staring at a triple chocolate cake topped with ice cream and sprinkles.

Just when I think to look up, I'm struck by another big question. What am I wearing? Last thing I remember I was topless and, well, pretty much wearing only my skimpy panties.

With one very shaky finger, I lift up the sheet that's covering us and find I'm wearing a t-shirt, most likely one of Pete's, and my underwear is still on, thank God! I sigh in relief and let the sheet drop. How the shirt got on me is still a mystery, but at least I don't have to cover up.

"Trying to sneak a peek? You never

cease to surprise me, Jenny. You're quite the little nympho, aren't you?" Pete chuckles. "Sorry to disappoint you though. None of that for you this morning. I'm cutting you off before you become too addicted."

I slap his chest and say, "Dick."

"See? I told you. You have a one track mind. No, you cannot have my dick this morning." And, of course, he laughs and it's a beautiful laugh, which irks me even more.

I was right. He's never going to let me live down this embarrassment. There's no way to avoid this conversation any longer because, embarrassed or not, I need answers. I look up and see him staring down at me with that irritatingly, sexy, stubbly smirk of his. He's got messy bed hair and there's a scratch on the wall by the door. Another memory comes back—flying stilettos.

In his other hand, the one that wasn't combing through my hair, he's holding a book. Reluctantly, I move over so that I'm no longer touching him. I move slowly to make a general assessment of my current physical state. Since I'm not feeling too queasy, I sit up in bed, pulling the sheets around me to cover my underwear. Being upright sends pounding pain into my head and I wince. Seeing my reaction, Pete places a bookmark in his book, closes it and places it on his chest before reaching over to his bedside table. Lucky book. I was there only moments ago and it was... nice.

Pete hands me a bottle of water and two little white pills. "Here. I thought you might need these this morning."

I take the water and pills from him, our fingers touching and bringing back memories from last night. Memories of entwined fingers, soft touches and passionate kisses. He must feel it too because his eyes dart to mine with an intensity that conveys too much and too little at once. Something happened last night, I can feel it. Something shifted, but I can't, for the life of me, remember what.

I swallow the pills and put the cap back on the bottle. My fingers pick at the label on the bottle nervously as I say, "Thanks. Um, Pete? Last night, did we...?" I purposefully leave the end of the sentence hanging. After everything else I said to him last night, I don't really want to say more this morning but I need answers. Pete shifts to lie on his side, head propped up on one hand.

"No, we didn't, and it's not because you weren't insistent, believe me. But no, we didn't."

I'm relieved yet disappointed at the same time. I feel so sick. I can barely ask, but I manage. "Why not? I mean, you could have. That's what you do, isn't it? Don't you usually..."

Pete gets up, tossing the sheet off of him. I'm trying very hard not to be distracted by the fact that he's standing there, wearing only a pair of boxer shorts and leaving way too little to the imagination. But that's not in the cards for us. Not anymore.

"Say it, Gina. Don't I usually fuck every woman I come across? Yes, that's exactly who I am and that's exactly what I do," he says angrily. He sounds like I offended him, but how? Maybe the truth hurts? Or maybe he's not really that person deep down inside and I've falsely accused him? Looks can be deceiving, look at me.

His voice drops, almost like an apology, "But not last night."

He starts rummaging through drawers, taking out pieces of clothing and putting them on. "It's time I brought you home. I'll give you some privacy so that you can get ready. I'll be down the hall in my study. First door on the right."

"Wait, Peter. I didn't mean to offend you, it's just that everything is still such a blur. In case you haven't noticed, I'm a bit of a train wreck right now and I'm trying to put all the missing pieces of last night together. I can't pretend that you constantly turning me down doesn't hurt, because it does, especially after what happened with my ex."

Pete leans on his dresser and looks down to the ground, hands stuffed in his pockets. Somehow, calling Anthony "my ex" makes it so real, so final. I was in a bad place last night and somehow, this morning things aren't so bad and it's mostly due to the man standing in front of me.

Despite the hurt he caused me, I need to let him know. "Listen, I was drunk last night and leaving with that guy. Who knows what could have happened to me but then you stepped in. I guess what I'm trying to say is, thank you. You saved me from making a whole lot of huge mistakes last night."

He flinches, as if I just slapped him but then his face relaxes into a sad smile. He walks back to the bed and leans down to place a hand on my cheek. Instinctually, I lean into his touch and he strokes my smooth skin with his thumb. Behind the cocky, arrogant, angry man, I see that there's someone caring and good trying to break free. He turned me down last night, but, in a way, he took care of me too. This is the third time he's stepped in when I was sort of shooting myself in the foot—okay, the head. Things would suck this morning if I was found at a frat house. If only Pete wasn't so messed up, I could see myself easily falling for this guy.

My mother's warning rings in my mind, *Don't fall in love with a Ferro.* That should be the mantra for every girl at her coming out ball.

Pete takes his hand away and his smile turns playful again. "You're welcome. Now, unless you're planning on riding on my bike wearing only panties and a tee shirt, which is perfectly fine with me by the way, I suggest you get yourself ready. Remember, first door on the right when you're done."

"Eeeeep!" I make a high pitched sound and slap my hands over my mouth. He's taking me home on his motorcycle? A little rush of excitement ignites inside of me and I do a small bounce on the bed. "Hmmm... I don't know. Clothing seems so drab and optional. Maybe we should christen that bike, me being a nympho and all." I give him a teasing smile and bite my lower lip, going for seductive again. Why can't I help myself from acting this way around him? Toxic flirting, all the fun and all the heartache wrapped into one. Maybe he's right and I am addicted.

Pete leans in, pushes my hair back to one side and whispers in my ear, causing goosebumps to erupt everywhere. Combined with the fact that I'm top shelf commando under the t-shirt and it is quite obvious what effect he has on me.

"What if I told you that it's already been christened?" He stands up straight, gives me a wink and walks out of the room.

I eye him, trying to side step him so my brights are out of sight. "Then there's not enough Lysol in the world—"

Pete takes my arm as I pass, and spins me around. His gaze dips before coming back to my eyes. "To what? Extinguish those twin towers of wantonness?"

My jaw drops. "Gentlemen do not

comment on when the ladies are cold!" I jerk my arm away, still shocked, jaw scraping the ground. I snap it shut and use my forearm to cover my headlights. "Twin towers of wantonness."

"Fine, hypnotic high beams in a too small t-shirt and with the curve of your ass just barely peeking out—which is sexy as hell, by the way—pretend you're not into me. Say it all you like, but I know the truth." His smile twists until one side is a little higher than the other. God he looks arrogant and totally lickable. Why does he have to fold his arms like that? Pete stands there, smirking at me.

"And what's that?" I mock, getting in his face a little bit. Dark stubble lines his jaw and spreads down his neck, but my gaze doesn't stray from his.

That's when he moves. The muscles in those strong arms barely brush against my t shirt when he moves to put his hands in his pockets. He does it slowly, watching my eyes the whole time. His bare forearm brushes over my brights. The touch is so light, barely there, and totally intentional.

The reaction is instant. I go ramrod straight and suck in air like I was sucker-punched.

Pete's smirk falls back into place. "That there's no amount of Lysol that will make your brights turn off, not when I'm around."

THE PEACOCK & THE MANDESK

August 10th, 10:45am

Last night I was too interested in other things to notice much about my surroundings. This morning is different. I look around the room to make sure I haven't forgotten anything and to take in the details before I go. His bedroom is downright luxurious and very masculine looking with deep rich colors.

It has a bit of an old world feel to it with intricate moldings at the ceiling with carved buttresses. There's a massive natural stone fireplace along the side wall with a plush rug in the center of the room dividing the space into a bed area and a sitting area. There's a king-sized bed with four massive wood posts, an in-suite bathroom that is practically bigger than the bedroom. But the thing that draws my attention the most is the antique high back lounge chair at one end of the room. It faces a huge floor-to-ceiling picture window that overlooks the Bay.

Next to the chair is a hardwood side table, where a couple of books are scattered. I walk over and scan the books, thinking I'll find current fiction, so I'm a little surprised to see the names such as William Butler Yeats, Walt Whitman, Oscar Wilde and John Donne, all poets, all classics. I remember seeing books of poetry in his study on that first night, but those are usually for show, to impress guests. Guests don't come in here. These are his. I run my finger along the cover, staring at the book, trying to connect it to the man and see how it fits in. He's looking for more. That's the only thing it tells me, and lingering will make me look too fan girl, so I drop my hand and walk away.

I've pretty much gathered up all of my things, except for last night's sexy outfit. I toss the lingerie, as well as the shoes, in the garbage bin because I never want to see them again. Last night was a mistake and I don't want any reminders. It's bad enough that the corset rubbed so hard in places that my skin is still tender. Swing dancing in a corset was stupid. Last night wasn't too intelligent either.

I look around for my stuff before I head out to find Pete in his study, but I don't see my purse. His quarters are massive. I get turned around walking down a hallway. This is nothing like our home, even though my family has money, it's not like this. I've never seen so many rooms dedicated to a son, and I know that Sean's rooms have to be even bigger and better since he's the first born.

"Pete?" I call his name and look down the hall and then back again. I'm looking more like my old self, wearing my plain jeans, simple white blouse and ballerina flats. I've tied my long hair into a low bun at the nape of my neck because if we're going to be riding on his motorcycle, I don't want to deal with a huge tangled mess when I get home.

"In here." His voice comes from the other end of the hall. I pad down the carpeted hall and quietly open the door.

He's sitting at his desk, reading and jotting down notes on a piece of paper, occasionally biting down on the tip of his pen. He hasn't noticed me yet, so I steal a couple of minutes to study him. He looks so relaxed sitting there. Not a trace of anger or smugness. As usual, his hair is a rumpled, floppy mess and he hasn't shaved yet, but the expression on his face is completely laid back and untroubled. As annoyingly attractive as he can be when he's being arrogant, not to mention how my insides stir when he gets angry, this version of him, the one I've woken up to, is heartening.

I stand in the doorway for a second. "Ah, the many sides of Peter Ferro. It's a shame he doesn't let this one show."

Pete looks up. Caution lines his face. He pushes up and walks toward me. "When a lion pretends he's a peacock, he doesn't last long."

I nod slowly, catching his meaning. "You sound a little fortune-cookie-ish there, Pete. You still have the issue that a peacock is not a lion, and at some point that bird is going to want to strut around with his badass plumage all over the henhouse, so you tell me—how long have you been writing poems?"

He stammers and takes half a step away from me. "I do not—" Pete reaches back, looking for his desk.

"It's right there, just another step back. I take his arm and lead him back the step. "It's okay. You can touch it. Your manly desk will help flood more testosterone into those veins. There you go." I pat his arms, teasing."

He grins down at me. "You can be such a—"

I get in his face, "A what?"

"An unimaginably, vivacious, and stunning know-it-all. Ballerina." Pete leans in, his nose nearly touching mine, and smirks.

"Why did you? Last night, I mean. It would have been on the up and up. Everyone saw me leave with you. There are a dozen messages, okay more, from Erin asking how it was to get nailed to the wall by Pete Ferro and for some reason, I get brushed aside."

"You were drunk."

"I'd made up my mind before we left, and not for nothing, but are you saying you've never nailed a drunk girl before?"

Pete watches me and I sense he's squirming beneath those beautiful blue eyes. "No."

"Why?" I'm not sure why this matters, but I have to know. Pete doesn't want to talk about it. He's shutting down and I doubt I'll get an answer, but I press him.

"Why what?"

"Why me? Or why not me? It seems like I'm not good enough or something, meanwhile every plastic chick within five miles of here has had you, but when it comes to sex and me—why?" Pete turns while I'm talking.

"Let's go for a ride."

"I have to know."

"Forget about it. Some things aren't worth knowing, and this one doesn't matter."

"That's for me to decide."

"Not if it's my secret, which it is."

I jump in front of him and smile huge. "You have a secret? About me? Any chance you wrote about it? In a poem?" Pete's lips twitch as he watches me. He's paused, not sure which way to go—to react charming or angry. Both defenses will throw me off balance and I'm expecting them. When neither comes and he just watches me, my stomach dips. "Pete? Did you write a poem?"

THE DOCTOR OF LOVE WILL SEE YOU NOW

August 10th, 11:06am

He rubs his hands over his arms and doesn't look away. His eyes are pinned on me, and his arms are folded in front, softly, like he's trying to hide a secret that wants to come out. His lips part as if he's going to tell me, but his phone buzzes. It breaks his trance. Pete looks down at it and then back up at me. "We better go."

I wonder who texted him, but he's already hidden the phone in his pocket.

"Okay, let me grab my things."

When I return with my coat, Pete is at his desk. He lifts the book he was reading, and marks his page. When he turns back, he stretches, which reveals a tiny bit of skin at the waist as the hem of his shirt rises. A small pang of regret hits me when I think of how last night and this morning went. I can't tell if I'm relieved or upset. Either way, sleeping in his arms felt different, safe. I haven't felt like that in a long time, like someone was watching out for me and would protect me. I want to take care of myself, but it's nice to have that feeling— even if it's not real.

Without a word, Peter stands and walks over to the couch, to retrieve the leather jacket that's laying on the backrest. I step towards the man desk and look at the notes he was jotting down. There are multiple technical notes about things like rhyme scheme, syllable count, writing structure and numerical patterns, but among those notes a quote stands out, written at the center of the page.

"Thus you may understand that love alone is the true seed of every merit in you, and of all acts for which you must atone."

-*Dante Alighieri, Purgatorio*

"Brushing up on your pickup lines this morning, I see." I tease, picking up the book and flipping through the pages.

Pete walks over to the desk, leather jacket in his hands and takes the book away from me.

"Very funny smart ass. If you must know, I was doing a doctorate in English literature. Reading books and analyzing them was part of the job."

I nudge him with an elbow. "I see. Put it like that and it sounds nearly respectable for a Ferro to become an artist."

"Very funny."

"No, seriously. I mean it. It must have taken Mother Ferro Dearest quite by surprise, but an artistic middle child is normal, expected even. So, how did you break it to her?"

"Break what?" Pete is watching me.

My lips slip into a smile. "That you were working on becoming a doctor of looooove?"

"Nice." He smirks and looks over at me.

"Trying to perfect the art of Don Juanisim?" I waggle my eyebrows at him.

"As if I needed to."

I laugh loudly, once. "Well, aren't we cocky?"

"Perhaps, but you're the one who keeps talking cock, not me. You mentioned it twice already—peacock and cocky. I think you have a fixation, Miss Granz."

"I think you have a bird phobia, Mr. Ferro."

He laughs and smooths his hair out of his eyes. "As if someone this manly could be afraid of something so small?"

"You get your evil powers from your man-desk, right? Are there testosterone packs in the drawers?"

"Smartass."

"I know you like my ass, but we don't need to talk about it. Come on, fess up. Why did you ditch the degree? Mama Ferro take away your allowance?" I grin up at him.

"Not quite. I quit before my dissertation. None of the profs here were offering projects I liked. To do a dissertation in poetry meant moving and that was not going to happen. Now if you are done with your insipid remarks, I'd like to get going."

"Hold on a moment." I touch the tip of my finger, like I just figured out something huge. "Just so I understand your way of thinking and why you do what you do— dancing is for pussies but poetry isn't?"

Pete smiles thoughtfully. "Laugh all you want, at least I was doing something I loved. Which is more than I can say about you. Don't make me believe for one second that you chose to study economics and business for your love of numbers. For some reason, I doubt that's what you really wanted to do."

Suddenly this conversation isn't funny. "How do you know about that?"

"I know many things."

"Wow," I blurt out without thinking. "You sound like your mother."

At that, his head snaps up and he walks straight to me. It's his intimidation stance but it has long lost its effect on me. "My mother? When did you talk to my mother? I told you to stay away from her. Damnit, Gina!"

I place a hand on his chest, hoping to get him to calm down. With a calm voice, I say, "Hey, it's okay, relax. It's not like I had a say in the matter, she tricked me into it. Besides, it was nothing. She was just offering me a job. Apparently, I'm good at numbers, even though it's slowly boring me into a slow and agonizing death. But I turned her offer down, so stop freaking out." This seems to pacify him, somewhat. He looks up at the ceiling and takes a deep breath. He's probably counting to ten, maybe twenty.

He calms his voice, intentionally speaking carefully. "Just try to avoid her from now on. With everything happening right now, I don't want you in her line of sight."

I search his eyes, but they don't give anything away. "What do you mean *with everything happening*? Pete? What *is* going on?"

He doesn't answer but hands me the jacket. "Here, put this on and let's go. You can leave your bag here. I'll have someone bring it to your house later."

BADASSERINA GINA

August 10th, 11:38am

Pete hands me one of the helmets. "Have you ever ridden on a motorcycle before?"

I shake my head. I put the helmet on and when he sees that I fumble with the chin strap, he silently offers to help. He pushes a button on the side of his helmet and on the side of mine and I hear a little blip in my ears. I blink in surprise.

Pete's voice comes through a set of speakers from inside the helmet, "Let me get on first and when I tell you to, you're going to put one foot here," he points to some kind of foot pedal thingy at the bottom, "hold onto my shoulders, and swing your other leg over to the other side. Got it?"

I nod, which is really weird with a heavy helmet on. I feel like a bobble head.

"Oh, and you can talk to me, I can hear you too." He gives me a quick little wink and sits on his bike. I stand there waiting, feeling a little bit awkward. He gets the motor going, which, in turn, gets mine going. Pete Ferro, on a motorcycle, revving the motor, is the epitome of manly and it's enough to make me want to go pull him back into the house and have my dirty way with him after all. Oh, and he knows what effect it has on the ladies too, because he looks at me when he revs the engine once more and his eyes light up wickedly.

When Pete tells me to get on, I follow his instructions and squirm, trying to get comfortable, which translates into trying to push my butt as far up on the seat as possible so that my lady parts aren't pressing up against his perfect butt. A very hard feat to accomplish seeing as the seat is on a forward slant and made of slippery leather.

Pete turns his head slightly to look over his shoulder. "I realize you have trouble controlling your little urges but I need you to sit still back there. Get as close to me as possible and no wiggling those sexy little hips of yours or we'll end up in a ditch, and not in the fun way."

"Ass." I try to be annoyed, but really, he's hot and he just said my hips were sexy. I can't get annoyed with that.

"Glad you're enjoying the view. Ready? Put your hands on my hips and hold on tight. Remember, no wiggling. When we turn, follow the bike, lean into the curve, not away."

"Got it." Oh my goodness! I can't believe I'm doing this. This is so cool!

When he takes, off, I'm taken by surprise by the jolt, and it sends me sliding backwards. I squeal and wrap my arms around his waist, holding on tight. Through the headphones in the helmet, I can hear Pete laugh. When we reach the end of the long driveway, he doesn't slow down to check for oncoming traffic, he just turns, the bike angling itself dangerously to the side.

"Follow the bike Gina! Lean into the curve." He warns as we're turning.

Easier said than done. My basic instinct for survival doesn't want me to lean towards the gritty asphalt that's coming closer and closer to my face with every passing moment. I like my skin and want to keep it on me, not leave it scraped in ribbons all over the road. I close my eyes and let myself go, letting my body tilt along with the bike. My grip around Pete's waist tightens and once we're back to being completely upright I start to breathe again, not realizing that I'd been holding my breath. I release my death grip around his waist but he places one hand over mine, entwining our fingers and gently squeezing, keeping me there. The angle of the bike has him laying down so low that I'm practically laying across his back.

"How was that?" He asks. I hear a smile in his voice. He obviously likes the rush.

"Oh my God! That was... amazing! Let's do that again." I giggle. I feel so alive. Pete laughs again, releases my hand and accelerates abruptly, making me squeal once more and hold onto him tighter.

The ride goes on for much longer than

it should, taking many detours and a couple of scenic routes, as opposed to the quicker, direct route. Being this close to Pete once more seems greedy, like asking for a 3rd helping of dessert but every time I go to release my grip on his waist, he does the same thing over and over again. He places a hand on mine and entwines our fingers until he needs to use both hands to maneuver his bike. We pass a truck carrying window panes and I catch our reflection in one of the glass sheets.

Oh, hell yeah, I'm so badass right now! Ha!

Pete laughs a genuine belly laugh and it's only then that I realize that I said that out loud and with the Bluetooth helmets, he heard everything. I don't care. This is too frickin' fantabulous.

We stop at a quaint little coffee house along the river to have a small late breakfast of coffee and warm, homemade donuts. He tells me more about his interrupted doctorate and it's obvious that he feels passionate about literature and poetry. I tell him all about dancing and being on stage. He listens attentively, not once referring to the fact that dancing is for pussies. We eventually get back on his bike and resume our ride. I keep asking him to go faster, to which he usually laughs and obliges willingly.

I wish this day could last forever but since all good things must come to an end, so does our little ride together. When the bike stops in front of my house, it's like waking up from a fantastic dream. The feeling is exhilarating. I can still feel the adrenaline pumping through my veins from some of the more dangerous turns and accelerations and I feel like I can fly.

We sit there for a couple of silent moments, my arms still wrapped around him, holding hands. "So," he says.

"So," I echo back, looking at his fingers. I want to hold onto the feeling but the dream is shattered when I see my mother and father, followed by Anthony, rushing out of the house.

Following Pete's instructions, I get off of the bike and he helps to unfasten the strap under my chin. I can't see all of Pete's face because of his helmet but I can see his eyes and when he spots Anthony, they narrow into slits and I know he's getting furious. I can see the anger gently bubbling up and I know what it ultimately means. I don't want him to fight. I don't want my stupid ex to affect his mood. He's been so happy and light hearted today and I want to keep him that way.

Thanks to the headsets, I know I can speak to him without the others listening in. "Peter, let it go. Please. He's not worth it."

I want to touch him so badly, to give him a comforting touch, knowing that it'll calm him down, but I can't. Not in front of my parents. Pete looks at me and his anger seems to subside a bit. When he doesn't say anything, I add, "Thank you, for everything."

I don't get to hear or see his reaction because my mother comes tearing down the steps, wailing, "Oh my dear heavens. Regina! You're safe! Where have you been? We've been worried sick!" My mother is in hysterics, and my father's voice booms out.

"Get in this house right now, young lady!"

Really? *Young lady?* Okay, so maybe shutting my phone off and not letting my parents know I was safe may not have been the smartest plan, but still. This is utterly embarrassing. Maybe I'll call Erin this afternoon and inquire about moving in with her. This would not have been an issue if I didn't live at home.

Anthony stays on the steps by the front door and doesn't come down. Before I get a chance to remove the helmet and the jacket, Pete revs the motor to his bike and takes off.

No goodbye, not even a nod.

He just leaves.

MANLY URGES

August 10th, 12:41pm

Pete's tail lights disappear and I hear a little blip, letting me know that our helmets are out of range. Everything gets eerily silent after that, except for the breeze rustling through the leaves, the distant sound of a lawn mower, and the happy chirping birds perched high up in the trees. Fucking birds.

I might as well get this over with. I'm not looking forward to crushing my parents' dreams when I tell them the truth about what happened. They are going to be so disappointed in Anthony.

I manage to remove the helmet and walk past everyone in silence, making my way towards the house. It's much too hot to keep the leather jacket on outside but I'm not ready to take it off just yet. The inside of the house is air conditioned, which will give me an extra little moment wrapped up in Pete's scent and of this morning's happy memories.

I can't believe the nerve of Anthony showing up here today after what he's done. When I storm past him on the front porch, I grit my teeth and say under my breath, so that only he can hear, "Why are you here? Run out of cat food?"

I don't wait to see his reaction. I simply walk into the house and head towards the living room. There's no sense in hiding in my room. They'll be up there like a cat up a tree in no time and, oh my God, why can't I stop thinking about freaking cats?

I take a seat on the couch and as soon as Anthony walks in, he takes the seat next to me, putting a hand on my knee. Before my parents have a chance to join us, I place my hand on his and squeeze it with all the strength I have, digging my nails into his skin. I see his face twist in pain and I say, "Don't ever touch me again, you lying, freaky, bastard!"

I let go of his hand and stand up, wanting to be as far away from him as possible. I'm consumed by rage and if he is anywhere near me, I may do something I'll regret. Legally, I'm not allowed to castrate anyone.

"Regina..." Anthony doesn't get a chance to continue because my father walks in, chest all puffed up like he usually does when he's about to reinstate discipline, followed by my mother, who's wiping a tear from her eye. The ticking of the grandfather clock is unusually loud as we wait for my dad's opening words. We don't talk before he does, not unless we are feeling suicidal. I can see a vein pulsating on his forehead. Yep! He's pissed alright. The Granz pulsating forehead vein is a measure of one's rage and right now, my Dad's has reached DEFCON 1. Guns are cocked and loaded and waiting to fire.

I'm concerned about his reaction when I tell him about his golden boy. He's not been feeling well and this will make him worse. If

Anthony wasn't here it'd be easier and a lot less tense.

Dad clears his throat, puts both hands behind his back and lifts his chin. "We're disappointed in you, Regina. Anthony called us last night, in a panic, saying that he couldn't find you anywhere, you don't answer your calls and then you show up the next morning on the back of some hoodlum's motorcycle? I didn't think my daughter was a cheap trollop. You've disgraced this family and betrayed Anthony's trust."

WHAT?

I take a deep breath and try to keep calm. Of course that's what they think, that I went off and did it with motorcycle man until dawn. This whole thing does look incriminating.

"This is not what you think. Yes, I should have called. That was my mistake, but there are some things you should know."

I look towards my ex, who's sitting quietly and much too relaxed for my taste. He should be shitting his pants by now. I'm about to out him in front of Reginald Granz the third, hardass extraordinaire and key master to his daughter's chastity belt. I put both hands in the pockets of Pete's leather jacket and take in a deep breath. "Anthony was unfaithful. I caught him with another woman last night. That's why I took off."

Dad runs a hand over his face and through his thinning hair. I'm waiting for him to go apeshit on Anthony's puny ass but instead he puts his hands on my shoulders.

He turns to me. In a creepy calm voice, he says, "Anthony told us everything. You can't jump to conclusions every time he decides to have dinner with a female classmate." Dad pats my shoulder like I'm an infant and can't tell what's what.

"Dinner? Is that what you're calling it now? Would you like me to tell you what he was really doing or are we going to continue on with this illusion of the truth?" I sound placid and perfectly regal. The problem is that it all falls apart.

My mom, always the pacifist, wanting to calm the troubled waters, pipes in, "Anthony explained it to us. He was only helping this young woman for their upcoming practical exam. Jealousy isn't very becoming, Regina.

Although I can understand how you must have felt. Running off is never the answer."

"Jealousy? Do you people even know what he did? No, of course not." I let out a sigh, not wanting to spell it out. "All right. Since you all seem to want to hash it out in the open like this, why not?" My hands are flying through the air while I speak. I'm not holding back anymore. If they want the truth, here it is. I point at my ex. "He cheated on me last night. As in he had sex with another woman, and there is no way to misinterpret anything because I saw it!"

My mom looks way too composed when she says, "Honey, maybe you just thought you saw something. They are doctors you know. Sometimes they need to practice physical examination techniques."

Oh holy hell. I blink at her. "Mom, how do you misinterpret something like seeing another woman's mouth sucking on my boyfriend's dick? I may not be a doctor but it seems to me that a demonstrating how to give a blow job isn't standard medical procedure!"

The grandfather clock keeps ticking away even though time seems to stand still. Mom covers her poor innocent ears, not wanting to hear about such vile things.

Anthony squirms in his seat and has his hands over his mouth, preventing himself from saying anything that may betray the truth, and my father is rubbing his eyes, probably unable to stand the look of me.

"Regina! You will watch your tongue in front of your mother!" His voice is high and clipped. His face is turning red and I know his heart rate is way up there. Stress is going to kill him one day and his little head will pop. Mom has told me how hard his job is over and over again. That's why I never want to add to the mess, but this is not okay.

"And not refute the accusation? Are you demented or did you order me from a website? Babies come from vaginas, not Storks-R-Us! I am very sorry I worried you but, that's the fact of the matter."

"NO." Dad's voice booms, cutting me off. "The facts are these: You acted like a child and stormed off when someone else looked at your toy the wrong way. Grow up, Regina. You can't have a fling every time someone hurts your feelings." He turns his gaze on Anthony. "As for you, so be it. These things happen from time to time."

"Sir, I—" Anthony tries to interrupt and

Dad turns beat red and stutters. It's as if he's gone into nuke mode and is about to blast off in front of us.

"However," Dad uses his huge voice and death glare to finish his statement without interruption, "if what my daughter says is true, let me give you a warning. Once you two are properly engaged, there is to be no more of this fooling around with other women."

Anthony hangs his head in shame and stares at the floor. Asshole.

"Regina," when he says my name, I flinch, "although your behavior last night was appalling, I'm willing to overlook it this once. I guess your mother should have prepared you more but please keep in mind that he is a young man and young men have..."

"Don't. Don't even say it, Dad. I swear to God if you say that young men have urges, I'm going to scream. That is such bullshit! It's a double standard. You're seriously justifying what he did because he's a guy? Yet you're condemning me for that exact same thing? News flash—I didn't do anything. Nothing happened! But you guys wouldn't know that because you never even bothered asking me!" By the time I'm done I know that nothing has gotten through. Daddy sees his little girl pitching a fit. It looks like a tantrum over a toy. I calm myself. "I'm sorry, but this should have been between me and Anthony."

He growls, "Regina Marie Granz, you will not use that tone with me if you know what is good for you. This whole mess could have been just between you, but you didn't answer your goddamn phone. If you want to be treated like an adult, then act like one.

"My business here is done. You two will sort out your differences so that we can all put this whole ugly affair behind us. And to ensure that neither one of you is tempted to do anything remotely stupid like this anymore, I'm going to help speed up this engagement. As of now, consider yourselves betrothed. I'll have the ring ordered and ready by the end of the week. We'll have the official engagement party before the end of the month. End of story." He smiles as he clasps his palms, like this is a happy event.

"Now if you will excuse me, I have more pressing business to attend to. It seems that while you were having your little lover's spat last night the final witness took a turn for the worst. They are keeping him on life support so that his family can say their last goodbyes. I expect that police are going to start making arrests fairly soon. I have to be sure that the company is ready to get through this potential media frenzy." Dad leaves the room, followed by my mom, who looks back over her shoulder with an apologetic look on her face.

I slump down on the chair in the corner of the room and pull my knees up to my chin, wrapping the jacket around me. I feel sick every time I think about it. Pete keeps saying it wasn't my fault, so does Erin, but I can't help but feel like that guy's life is on my shoulders. I deserve to go to jail. I nearly blurt out the whole thing, but I can't—not with Anthony here—and not with Daddy already worked up. One day I'm going to blurt something out that knocks the wind out of him. That vein will throb one too many times and burst. It happens to men his age with this kind of pressure. He has to maintain past traditions while embracing the future, and all while continuing to grow the family fortune. Some men have lost everything they had from one wrong move.

It's like playing chess with a child—the game can end at any time, for any reason, without reason. I feel like I'm the straw, the piece that cracked the whole damn camel.

Anthony clears his throat. I can't believe he's still here.

"Anthony?"

"Yeah, baby?"

"Go cough up a furball."

FLAME OUT

August 13th, 12:46pm

Fourteen minutes to go before my lunch break ends and I'll be officially late for work.

The wind whips my coat open and I clutch it tightly. A car horn blares somewhere behind me as I hurry up.

I had to invent an excuse so that no one would come looking for me. After last weekend's events, my father has become overly protective—that's the nice way of saying it. He thinks I'm trashing it up with my stash of lovers that I keep hidden in every part of the city.

Irony is a bitch.

No one knows where I am right now, and I want to keep it this way. Coming here is a stupid idea, I know, I should stay away but I can't help myself. I had to come. I had to see for myself and apologize in person.

I pull my phone out from Pete's leather jacket and start to key in a message to Charlotte.

Running an important errand. I'll be late coming back from lunch. Hold all my calls plz.

As I type, I'm distracted by the glittering diamond on my left hand. It shines brightly despite the lack of sunlight. It's not real. That's what I keep telling myself even though my loser list is getting bigger by the second.

I'm still debating how I should tell my dad that this wedding will never happen. Anthony and I haven't seen each other since last Saturday at my parents' house and I have no intention whatsoever of seeing him again—at least not until our engagement party. Until then, I'm just waiting to see how the next couple of days will unfold.

A bird screeches as it streaks overhead.

The air is damp this afternoon, like it might rain. My feet sink into the grass as I cross the cemetery, trying to hang back from the group. The truth is, that it didn't take long for the young man, the last witness, to pass away once life support had been turned off. According to what I overheard between my father and the detective, his body went straight to autopsy to confirm cause of death and now the police have all the evidence they need to make their arrests.

They have some names, one of them being the deceased, but he's gone now. As for me, so far, all has been surprisingly quiet. No one has come knocking on my door with handcuffs. No one blames me, even though I feel guilty.

My phone vibrates in my hand. Charlotte is quick to reply, confirming that she got my message and to take my time. I tuck my cell back safely in an inside pocket.

The atmosphere is quiet and somber and the sky is appropriately gray, threatening to open up at any moment. I stand there, hiding behind a massive, century old oak tree hoping that no one will see me. I can hear the sounds of people sobbing in the distance and see them hugging each other, all dressed in black. They toss flowers on a slowly descending casket.

A chill goes up my spine and I wrap the black leather jacket around me tighter, taking in its comforting smell and warmth. It's as if Mother Nature knows when life takes a bad turn. It's not supposed to be chilly this time of year. Fall is still a couple of weeks away and the leaves in the trees are still very green, but I feel so cold, right down to the bone. To think that could have been me. If it wasn't for Pete's heroic gesture, I'd be dead. A cold, lifeless corpse being lowered into the ground. Pete could have saved him that night but instead, he chose to save me. I got a second chance at life and I'm no better off today than I was before any of this ever happened. In fact, it seems like my life is less and less my own with every passing day.

My fingers flick at the engagement ring around my finger, not used to its presence. Dad insists that I wear it all the time as a reminder of where my loyalties lie. I think he's hoping that it'll be a man repellant. See a girl with an engagement ring and walk the other way. To me, the ring feels more like a concrete weight, pulling me down.

And to think, if I had decided to not go through with this stupid party in the first place, these people wouldn't be grieving his loss. That's the cruelest part of death. It's those who are left behind that will ache forever because I made that one decision.

One soul has been taken away and many more have been shattered by grief.

My legs can't stand the weight of the world anymore. That could have been me. It could have been Erin—or Pete.

Pete.

He ran in to save me. God! I grip my face and want to scream, but can't. I'm trapped all the time, everywhere. I fall to my knees and lean against the tree, hoping that it will be strong enough to keep me up.

Resting my head against the rough bark and wiping the tears from my eyes with the backs of my hands. "I'm sorry." I whisper, hoping that he can somehow hear me.

People start to leave, entering nearby cars or walking away through the cemetery gates with their heads down and shoulders slumped. I watch until there are only two people left standing next to the hole in the ground.

A young woman with bright red hair is

crying uncontrollably, her face in her hands, and a man, tall with dark hair and built. The man is standing behind the woman and looks defeated.

Peter.

My heart aches, because I want to go to him. I want to ease whatever that look is and make it never come back. I wonder if he had to choose between me and his friend. OMG! What if that's his best friend?

The woman is also familiar. I also recognize her after a few moments. She's the one Pete was with that night at the warehouse. I have caused so much damage already, I should leave them in peace and get back to work. The thing is, I can't look away. It's like watching two cars collide and waiting for the sound of broken glass and screeching tires.

Pete walks closer to her and puts a hand on her shoulder. When she turns around, it looks like he's trying to say something. She shakes her head and pushes him roughly. He tries to say something else, putting his hands on her shoulders, but she shakes him off.

The conversation seems to be getting heated but I can't quite hear what they are saying; only that she is screaming and he is trying to calm her down.

I stand up and get closer, trying not to be seen, making my way behind trees, bushes, and tall headstones. Stealth-mode Jenny. She shoves him with both hands on his chest but he doesn't budge.

As I get closer, her words are clearer. "This is all your fault! If it wasn't for you, he'd still be alive."

Pete is restraining her, holding her by the wrists, preventing her from hitting him again. He doesn't say anything and his eyes are cold, almost unfeeling. The longer he holds her, the more livid she gets. Her hair is flying in every direction like wild fire, caught in the wind.

I can't let Pete take the blame for this. This is my fault. I'm the reason he died, not Pete. He didn't get to him on time because he saved me instead. My life was spared at the expense of his. "Stop! It's not his fault!" Before I realize what I'm doing, I step out from where I'm hiding and walk closer to them.

Pete's eyes cut to mine in disbelief and lets the girl's wrists go.

The woman looks at me with a vile sneer and bloodshot eyes. She steps closer to me and looks back and forth between Pete and I as she does. "Who's this, Pete? Your new little toy?" She looks me up and down in disgust, like she can't comprehend why I'm even allowed to breathe the same air as her.

I walk closer toward Pete but he puts his hand out to stop me. "No. She's nobody. Just an insignificant nuisance that won't go away." He says it with hatred in his voice, looking straight at me. If he'd reached into my chest and pulled out my heart, it would have been less painful.

I know we're not anything to each other, we can't be, not in any romantic way. I'm engaged now and he's not that kind of man, but to say that I'm *nobody, a nuisance*? I would have liked to think that we were, at the very least, friends. Why is he doing this? I'm trying to help him and he's hurting me.

The redhead keeps on staring at us as if she's listening in on a private conversation and her sneer gets wider. She walks up to Pete and rakes her nails across his chest. He just stands there, seething, his fists clenched, his gaze never leaving mine.

"Right. Well, just so you know, this isn't over. I am going to make you pay for this,

Ferro. You can count on it." She looks me up and down one last time and turns on her heels before she storms off, leaving Pete and I alone in the cemetery.

IN THE SHADOWS

August 13th, 1:03pm

My fingers nervously play with the zipper at the bottom of his jacket. When I finally decide to say something, he doesn't let me. As soon as I open my mouth to speak, Pete grabs me by the hand and leads me towards the far end of the cemetery. I'm not what you would call tall, so for every step Pete takes, I have to take three. He's walking while I'm practically running just to keep up.

We end up behind a mausoleum that is

partly hidden by trees and bushes. He pushes me up against the stone wall and cages me in by placing a hand on either side of me. His temper has not died down. If he was a cartoon character, steam would be coming out of his ears accompanied by the sound of a steam train whistle.

"What are you doing here, Gina? I thought I asked you to keep a low profile. You shouldn't be here." It comes out like a yell, but I don't flinch. I just look into those heated blue eyes and try to see the calm beyond the storm that is raging inside. I know it's there, I've seen it.

"A better question is, what are you doing here, little brother?" A deep voice cuts through the air and makes me jump. When I whirl around, Sean Ferro is standing there in a dark coat, his lips pressed into a thin line. "You can't keep yourself out of trouble, can you?"

Pete looks him over in an adversarial way. It's the dumb ass guy posturing thing. Pete puffs up and I know he wants to hit something. Red pissed him off and he's mad that I'm here, now his brother shows up. Pete flexes his hand and then growls at Sean, "I'm not you. I won't end up dragging this family's name through the mud the way you did either."

"Of course. It was all intentional." Sean's voice is cold, callus.

Pete laughs bitterly. "The Ferro mantra —there are no mistakes. Is that what you're saying Sean? Because I thought there was no way you'd be walking away from that trial and yet here you are."

They stare at each other for a moment. I can't stand the silence, so I speak. "I can leave you guys alone. I'm supposed to be somewhere else, anyway."

"Gina, wait." Pete's tone is sharp, like he's not done scolding me.

"I'm the one who's departing, I'm afraid. I thought I'd tell Peter—"

"Don't call me that. We're not kids anymore. I'm not Peter and you're not Seanie. If you'd stop being so damn cryptic your counsel could have ended the trial before it began." Pete is in a standoff pose, mirroring his brother.

"Thanks for that. I hadn't known." Sean's voice is tense. He glances side to side and takes a step closer. "I came here for a reason. I'm leaving. Jon was—"

Pete smirks and looks at me. "He's

running. I can't believe it—the great Sean Ferro has fallen. You were supposed to run before the trial, dumbass."

Sean remains rigid. "Jon has something going on. Talk to him and keep him out of trouble. I'll be back when I can. Oh, and here—give this to Mom. The legal team has copies that will be delivered tomorrow. I thought you'd want to know now." Sean reaches out with an envelope in his hand. Pete doesn't move to accept it. Sean tosses it at Pete's feet and hisses, "It changes nothing. You're still the heir whether you take the paper or not. Have a nice life, Peter."

"I will if I avoid you."

Sean stiffens. I think he's going to be angry, but he just nods, turns on his heel, and leaves. In a matter of seconds he disappears into the back of a black car and bolts.

"Pete, he sounded like he was leaving and you told him to screw off? Did you mean to do that?" Bending down, I pick up the letter. I mock his voice, "You should open that, Gina." I make my voice higher, "Okay, Pete. I bet there's a dollar in here! Dibs!"

Pete snort-laughs and swipes the paper out of my hands. "You're an ass."

"So are you, but we both know that. Open the letter. Did he seriously just walk away from the family? Did your mom disown him?" As I ask, Pete opens the seal and scans the contents.

After a moment, he swallows hard, and looks up. "No, he's walking away from us."

"Which means you're the new Ferro heir. Can he do that?" I grab the letter and look at the lawyers names on the bottom, wondering if he can really do that. No one walks away from wealth and power. And why now? "It's weird."

Pete snatches it back. "Yes, it is, and it looks like he can leave whenever he wants. I just didn't expect him to do it."

"Looks like you were wrong about that."

We both stare at where the car used to be, as if a shadow of it were still there. "He'll be back. Family is everything. There's no way he's gone."

"Pete, he lost his family—his wife is gone. I don't think he was messing with you. I think he really left."

"No way. He'll be back." Pete glares at me. "Why did you come? This was stupid."

"You sound like Sean."

"You didn't answer the question." He's not amused with my answer.

"Fine. I needed closure. I needed to be here today. I would have left, but I saw you and then that woman started yelling." I glance up at him and look back at the grave. "And she was wrong. This isn't your fault, it's mine." I place a hand on his cheek and his eyelids lower. His body relaxes and I can see the tension start to melt away.

He places his hand over mine and gives it a gentle squeeze. Just when I think I've been able to help him get through this fit of rage, his body tenses once more. His eyes spring open and he removes my hand from his cheek and studies it, his gaze getting cold and menacing again.

"What's this?" His thumb brushes over the diamond on my left ring finger.

I shrug. "Cruel and unusual punishment for showing up that morning with you. It's man repellant." I remove my hand from his and hide it my pocket.

"He proposed and you accepted? After what he did to you? Why would you do something like that?" He's back to yelling at me, this time, pacing back and forth in front of me and pulling at his hair with his hands.

I'm too tired to get angry. "He didn't propose. My father slapped the ring on my finger and told us point blank that Anthony and I were engaged." I kick a small stone and it hits one of his black leather biker boots. "And to think some people say that romance is dead. What do they know? By the way, the party is in two weeks. Invitations are in the mail. It's black tie and try not to screw any of the guests this time. Hey! Want to be my date at my engagement party? We could shock the knickers off of my mother."

Pete stops his pacing and looks up at me, his lips curling up on one side, making his dimple reappear. "Wiseass. So, let me get this straight. Your father forces you into an engagement and you simply did as you were told? You didn't argue with him? That doesn't seem like you at all, Jenny." He tsks with his tongue and shakes in head in mock disapproval. "I'm disappointed in you. You're losing your touch." A hint of mirth glints in his eyes as he says it.

Pete rests his back on the wall next to me, letting out a rush of air and looking up toward the canopy of trees above our head.

"You shouldn't be here, Gina. It was reckless. In fact, you shouldn't be seen with me either. It's better if we don't see each other again."

"Is it because I'm engaged or because I'm an insignificant nuisance that won't go away?"

He doesn't answer me, probably meaning that it's a little bit of both. His head drops and I start to take off the leather jacket, letting it slip from my shoulders. "Here, this is yours. Thank you for letting me borrow it."

Pete puts a hand on my arm, stopping me from removing the jacket. With a sad smile he says, "Keep it. I kinda like it on you. It makes you look like the tough little chick I know you really are." Pete pushes himself off of the wall and slips the coat back over my shoulders. He drops a kiss on the top of my head and gives my chin a small pinch in between his thumb and finger and says, "Goodbye, Gina."

LIGHTNING IN A BOTTLE

August 17th, 2:11pm

"Regina, sweetie, may I come in?" Mom opens the door to my room just a crack and pokes her head in. I'm sitting on my bed, crossed-legged with my laptop glowing in front of me.

It's been four days since the funeral and everything has been eerily quiet. It's funny how slowly time goes by when you're waiting for impending doom to come crashing down. Even so, I turned in my final reports for my internship. Daddy has kept me on staff full time until the Fall semester starts. I'm still debating if this is due to my exceptional number crunching skills or if it's to babysit me. Going into the last year of my BBA should sound exciting but right now I can't seem to grasp the notion. In nine months I'll be graduating and most likely heading to graduate school. That seems so far away right now, like a lifetime away. Based on the way my parents reacted the other night, I don't know if it's even worth it.

Periodically I catch a reflection of myself in my parent's eyes and it makes me cringe. They see a weak, giddy, little girl who can't take care of herself. Well, maybe not Mother, but Daddy sees nothing more. It felt like a sucker punch to the stomach when he didn't believe me, side with me, or offer anything in the way of support regarding Anthony. Meanwhile, I'm the deranged one because I still want to see that beaming face that he wears when he's happy with me. Is it bad to want their affirmation? Because I do. It's not that I'm weak, but there are so many choices and a million more variables that accompany each decision. Sometimes I just want to know that I'm on the right track.

This isn't my path, but I can't stop wondering about him. I take one last look at the picture of those beautiful, bitter blue eyes staring at me from the computer screen, and shut the lid.

Pete's been in the news a lot over the past forty-eight hours. What Sean said in the cemetery was true—he left the family fortune behind and Pete is the new heir. No one has seen Sean since the night he took off. That means me and Pete were the last people to see him before he vanished. Maybe I'm a nutjob for thinking it, but I feel bad for Sean. I never really thought he did anything they accused him of, but seeing him in person made me more certain. He has that same look in his eye that Pete's had lately. It's not their normal arrogance, it's more like the panicked eyes of a lost child.

No one was kind to Sean, not even his brother.

And again, I did nothing. I'm not kinder or any different than I was before the fire. I want to change. I want it so bad, but when it comes to following through, I suck at it. How hard would it have been to smile at the guy? Or say something assuring or sweet?

No wonder why people don't change. Even if they want to, it's incredibly difficult to actually do it. At least it is for me. Pete, on the other hand, jumped into his new role as heir pretty quickly. The media is going wild with this information, trying to poke their noses into Pete's personal life, getting all the gritty details behind the man who is now the newest, most eligible wealthy bachelor.

My mind bounces back to the other night with Pete and all those warnings to stay away from him and his mother. He said to keep a low profile and not get myself tangled in their mess. Maybe he meant this stuff with Sean?

I'm not certain, but I can't help but feel sad for Pete in light of the news. He is like a wild animal, uncaged and untamed to the point that I envy him. To become the heir of such an enormous fortune has its responsibilities. It'll be like putting him in shackles. I know because I've been wearing mine every day since the day I was born.

My mother almost died giving birth to me and it was clear after that traumatic experience that my parents would not be able to have any more children. I think that my dad was secretly hoping for a son, so he could pass down the family name— Reginald Granz the fourth—who would eventually run his company. Instead, he had to settle for a Regina. Being a single child had its perks. I was always Daddy's little princess, got all their love and attention, and was spoiled, but I was also overprotected. What would become of the family line should something happen to the sole heir? Massive bickering as family comes out of the woodwork like snakes, decimating what remains of the estate. It's every father's nightmare, but now it's Pete's nightmare too since Sean left.

I fake a smile at my mother. "Hello, Mother. What can I do for you?" She walks into my room and has a worried expression on her face.

"Your father would like to see you downstairs in his office. He said it was urgent." She squeezes her hands once before loosening her grip. She's nervous and doesn't want me to see. "I think you better get down there quickly. He has important company with him so it's best not to keep them waiting."

The pit of my stomach goes into a

freefall as I try to swallow past the lump in my throat. They know. They know about the fire and the party. They know I let people in and ruined everything. After I find enough air to speak, I nod and say, "Tell Dad I'll be down there in a minute."

As I go to stand up, my mother takes a seat next to me on my bed. She puts a hand on my knee. Her eyes search mine and I know she sees everything. My mother has a way of seeing through me. It's insane how well she knows me. "Gina, darling, that man the other day, the one on the motorcycle? It was Peter Ferro, wasn't it?"

My heart lurches and jumps off a cliff too. Great, where is this conversation going? I don't look up. "What does it matter?"

"It matters because you care for him, don't you?" Her tone is soft but cautious. She tips her head to the side, trying to catch my eye.

My answer is equally cautious. There's no point in entertaining the *what if's*. Pete's message was clear. He doesn't want to see me again and in light of recent events, I'm starting to understand why. "It doesn't matter much, but I might care about him. The thing is, I think there's more to him.

He's not the bad person people think he is, Mom. He's a good person with a bad rep." I'm picking at the diamond on my engagement ring as I talk.

They don't know about all the times he's stepped in to help me. They just see the surly, angry young man who leaves a path of destruction everywhere he goes.

Mom is silent for a while before she replies. "Just remember what I told you before." She strokes my hair and puts her hand under my chin, lifting it up so I can look at her. "The Ferro boys can be intensely captivating, but when it comes to trying to get them to love you back, it's like trying to catch lightning in a bottle—highly dangerous and nearly impossible. I know you and Anthony are going through a rough patch, but if you stick with him I think you'll be happy. He'll be a steady husband." She smiles and lets out a small laugh. "And if he's not, you'll whip him into it, I'm sure. Now, get ready and come meet us downstairs in the office." She gives me a comforting smile and a kiss on the cheek before getting up and leaving me alone once more.

WTF?!?

August 17th, 2:29pm

I'm standing just outside the door to my father's office. My hand is on the doorknob, trembling. When my mental countdown gets to zero, I take in a deep breath and open the door.

I'm not surprised to see my father sitting behind his desk, scowling, and my mother sitting in one of the chairs. She's twisting a handkerchief in her hands.

I am surprised, however, to see that my father's guests aren't the cops at all. They are none other than Mrs. Ferro and...

"Pete?"

Was this why my mom was asking me about him? Wanting to know how I felt about him? I was so certain that I'd never see him again. Hope rises up in my chest as I imagine all the different reasons why he would be here with his mother.

My hopes fade quickly when I look at him. Pete is standing by the window, looking disheveled and beautifully unkempt. He also looks tired, with dark circles under his very cold and unfeeling eyes. Something isn't right, which makes my blood turn to ice.

Mrs. Ferro looks between the two of us and starts to talk with a strictly business, no-nonsense tone. "Wonderful. We don't have to pretend that you don't already know each other. That'll make everything so much easier. Now if we can get down to business. Please, Miss Granz, why don't you have a seat so that we can get started?"

I look over at my dad, who is leaning back in his chair, arms crossed and forehead vein pulsating. Crap. His face is red and he's totally pissed. Again. I'm going to give him a coronary. Maybe it's not me this time, but I have a sinking feeling it is. Daddy doesn't like to have someone else overstep his authority in his house, especially not a woman. Seeing as Mrs. Ferro has the seat of power, you know the chair that everyone else faces that's a little higher and bigger than the rest—that's where she's sitting. Daddy is across from her, not liking it. We all know that messing with Mrs. Ferro is like taunting Satan. Everyone wants to know her, but no one actually wants the woman in their home.

Yet, Daddy sits there, brooding, with Mrs. Ferro in his chair. This is going to suck.

I slowly make my way to one of the chairs and sit down quietly next to my mom. Ankles crossed, tucked back, hands placed lightly on my lap, spine straight, plastic smile. Gina is ready for this high society face off. Sometimes I think it'd be easier if we just bitchslapped each other—like now.

Mrs. Ferro jumps in. "Let's not skirt the matter and make this more drawn out than it needs to be." Pete's mom sneers at the tea cup in her hand, grimacing as if it were made from cow patties. It's a vintage Tiffany's pattern from the turn of the last century and cost more than a car, but apparently that's not good enough for her.

She's making it clear that we are not her peer group. None of us are good enough for her. She continues, "Mr. Granz, I realize you are a busy man but I have important matters to discuss with you; matters that will have great impact on both our families. I understand that you are waiting upon the arrest of the culprits responsible for the fire that occurred at your warehouse a couple of months ago. I also heard the final witness passed away."

My dad shifts in his chair, obviously annoyed. "I am not at liberty to discuss such matters, Mrs. Ferro. All the information is in the hands of the detectives. A public statement will be issued when the time is right, until then—"

"No, that is where you are wrong, Mr. Granz." Mrs. Ferro interrupts my father and opens a designer leather briefcase that's resting by the foot of her chair and pulls out two thick file folders, each held closed by thick elastic bands. "All the information is in my hands, not the detectives'. I have here the files for two of the suspects that the police were going to arrest. You may find this one particularly enlightening."

Mrs. Ferro hands one of the folders to my father and my heart stops beating. I don't see what is written on the papers, but I'm pretty sure I know the contents. My palms get sweaty and my gaze travels over to Pete, who is still standing, expressionless and cold.

Soon he'll know what I've done. They all will.

Poor Pete. Will he regret having saved me when he finds out that it was all my doing in the first place? Another question bubbles up to the surface.

Why does Mrs. Ferro have my file? How'd she get it to begin with?

Dad's face goes white, but he doesn't say anything. That freaking vein is enough to tell me that he knows. He puts the contents back in the envelope and wordlessly hands it to my mother. Dad looks at me with knives in his eyes. I glance away, to my mother, who is examining the contents of the envelope.

In a clear plastic bag, I can see my old cell phone, cracked and charred but the metal backing clearly engraved with my name and my fingerprints visibly marked all over. In another bag are a handful of pearls from my old necklace, also marked with my prints from all those times that I nervously rolled them between my fingers. My mother looks at the paperwork with my name in big, bold letters.

After she puts the contents back in the envelope, she hands it back to Mrs. Ferro with confusion pinching her face. "I don't understand, Constance. What does our daughter have to do with any of this?"

When no one answers, I turn to her and take her hand. "Mom, Dad, I'm so sorry. I gave them access to the building for the rave. I had no clue things were going to turn out this way. It seemed so harmless at the time. Just a bunch of us having fun. I thought the warehouse would be safe." My mom lets out a sob and covers her mouth.

Dad completely disregards what I said and pretends like I'm not even in the room. He just stares at Mrs. Ferro through slitted eyes.

"And what would you like from us?" My mother's voice is cool and even. She's playing the game, step by step, and I know her heart is breaking because of what I did. I want to blurt my heart out, but I can't— not now.

"I was hoping we could come to an agreement, seeing as we are both in the same mess." She sends a menacing look over to Pete, tapping the second file in her hands. On the front it clearly reads "Peter Ferro."

I stand up abruptly. That can't be right. Two and two slam together and I get it. "Wait, that's not right! Peter didn't do anything wrong! In fact, he saved me. If it wasn't for him, I'd be dead! He risked his life to get me out of that building, and then he took care of me, made sure I was safe. He's a good man. You can't blame him for any of this. All this is my fault. All of it!" I'm frantic. I'm looking at everyone in the room but no one seems to be listening to me, not even Pete. I walk up to him and put my hands on his arm. "Pete. Tell them that you saved me. You ran into the fire and got me out. Tell them!"

"Gina, don't." Pete shakes me off and offers a frightening look, like the bomb hasn't dropped yet.

They are holding something back. Something horrible. I can feel it.

"How endearing. My son, the hero. Well, Miss Granz, don't hold your expectations of him too high. He may not be as valiant as you think." As his mother speaks, Peter looks at me waiting to see my reaction.

Shaking my head, my lips curl into my denial smile. "There's nothing you can say that will prove he didn't. I know he saved me that night."

"He may have been the one to pull you out of that building, indeed saving your life. However he's the one who almost killed you in first place."

A WHAT-NOW?

August 17th, 2:41pm

"What?" This makes no sense. My mind is going around in circles, trying to put pieces back together. I planned the party. Pete was there. Why would she even think that?

I try to search his eyes but he's closed himself off completely, so nothing can get to him. It's only when Mrs. Ferro starts to talk again that I can look away from him and when I do, he walks away to the far end of the room, putting as much distance between us as possible.

"Don't be so quick to defend him, Miss Granz." Pete's mother speaks with authority and certainty. There's also an undertone that's scary as hell, like there's more to come and this isn't the worst of it. "As commendable as my son's actions were, I cannot overlook his sin."

"His sin?"

"Yes, Miss Granz. Peter's the one who set the place on fire."

"No, he couldn't have. That was that other guy. The one who passed away. He started the fire. I, I don't... Pete?" I stutter as my legs go numb and my cheeks start to prickle, like I'm about to faint. I have to sit on the edge of the deep windowsill otherwise I'll fall over.

Although I want her to shut up, to stop saying words that are destroying me bit by bit, Mrs. Ferro just keeps on talking, with a tone that's bordering on boredom and annoyance, while my father sits there in silence, nostrils flaring and looking at me with the most vile and condemning look I've ever seen.

"There were multiple witnesses who saw my son having illicit relations with a woman.

It appears that this woman was already spoken for and her other half retaliated. My son, being the gentleman that he is, beat him to near unconsciousness. He was the young man who passed away this week."

"No, he didn't." I squeak, my voice too high.

Pete's back is turned to me and he's looking up towards the ceiling, arms crossed in front of him.

Mrs. Ferro continues her explanation, ignoring me. "According to witnesses, during the brawl, many candles were knocked over, some accidentally, some—" she looks towards Pete, "not entirely by accident. It didn't take long for the flames to set fire to the nearby drapes and my brave son, seeing what was happening, up and ran. He's no hero."

"But, he didn't leave. He saved me." My voice trails off.

It's only then that Pete turns around and speaks up, his voice is as cold and unfeeling as his eyes. "Stop it, Gina. I did leave. It's only when I got to my car that I remembered you were up in that storage room and do you know why I remembered?" I slowly shake my head, not certain I want an answer, but he gives it to me anyway. "I saw you run up those stairs after I caught you looking at us and I had every intention of going up there and fucking you up against a wall, just like you'd seen me do to that other woman. Don't think it had anything to do with being brave or heroic. I knew you were up there because I sent you running. I didn't want bodies."

"Yes, except for the poor son of a bitch you knocked out." His mother smiles at him coldly.

The world around me slows. I hear my mother gasp at the same time Mrs. Ferro spits out her words, but I can't bring myself to react. A myriad of emotions whirl around inside of me. Sadness turns to heartbreak, which turns to anger and boils into utter hatred.

My fists clench and I hurdle myself at him. "You son of a bitch!" Before I know it, my fist goes flying and connects with his jaw. Unfortunately, I'm a righty, not a lefty. That huge ass rock on my left hand could have caused some major damage to that freakishly pretty face of his.

He doesn't stop me from hitting him on the first punch but when I go for another, he grabs my wrist and tosses it back. Pete takes a step closer. We're standing toe to toe. He's towering over me, but my rage makes me feel ten feet tall.

"All this time, you've just been easing a guilty conscience! How dare you, you sick, sorry excuse for a human being!"

Pete looks down at me. "Yes, I am. But we all knew that from day one, didn't we Mother?"

"Do not blame me for your barbaric actions. It's been bad enough dealing with your brother, and now this." Mrs. Ferro keeps her tone level and lethal as she scolds Pete. "You have no one to blame for this except yourself and you damn well know it or you wouldn't be here."

Everyone goes quiet and it becomes clear that my mother is crying into her handkerchief. My stomach twists. I want to make it better. This has to stop without ripping them apart. Pete is back to standing at the window, while my father and Mrs. Ferro glare at each other like they are locked in a staring contest.

My father breaks the silence. "Why are we all here if you already know about the arrests? He goes to jail where he obviously belongs, my daughter" he says *daughter* as if it leaves a foul taste in his mouth, "gets severe criminal charges laid against her and probably serves time as well. What's your interest in all of this? What do you want?"

Mrs. Ferro leans forward in her seat, like she's been waiting for this moment for a long time. "The future of Granz Textiles is at stake. Before all of this," she motions to the stacks of police reports as if they were disease ridden, "came out, we were in the middle of a corporate takeover. I'm surprised that you didn't see it coming. You should have listened to your daughter, Mr. Granz. You underestimate her capabilities. She had us worried there for a moment when she noticed our stockbroker buying into your stock but you completely disregarded her warnings."

My heart sinks further. I blurt out what I'd thought was happening. "You were planning a creeping tender offer, weren't you? Buying enough stock to have management control of the company? That's how you were going to do it." I can't believe it. I was right.

I wish I'd been wrong.

"Yes, Miss Granz. We want to own the

rights to that new patent of yours and as we currently stand, we own enough stock to take over the company and do as we wish. Our original plan was to sell off Granz Textiles, bit by bit, keeping the parts that were of interest to us. Now, in light of everything that's happened, we have a different proposition."

The room is sucked into silence. All eyes are on Pete's mom and she's got that killer smile of triumph across her face. We're all fucked.

Constance continues, "If you agree, we can make all the charges laid against both Peter and Regina disappear and silence the witnesses. It will be as if nothing ever happened and, as an added bonus, we will keep Granz Textiles intact. So, it will remain in your family, to some extent. Say no, and Peter goes to jail, Miss Granz ends up with heavy criminal charges, possibly jail time as well, and Granz Textiles belongs to us completely, to do with it as we will."

Something doesn't mesh. Before my father can answer, I speak up. "You're lying. Something is missing. You haven't said part of what you want, I can tell. If you have the power to make all of this go away, to buy the witness' silence, keep Pete out of jail AND take over Granz Textiles, why don't you? You don't need us."

Daddy snaps his fingers at me, but I don't stop talking. "Regina."

"What do we have that you want so badly and that you can't get without our consent?"

"Regina!" Father yells, "Enough!"

Mrs. Ferro disregards my father's outburst completely and gives me a glance that could be the closest thing to admiration I've ever seen from her. Her brow lifts and I can practically hear her thinking *smart girl.* "You are very shrewd, Miss Granz, and I admire your strength of character."

Every little bit of her is conniving and strategic. Every word that drips from her mouth is bait set in a trap and I'm determined not to fall into it, that is, until she answers my question, "I also admire your sense of loyalty. You want to know what you have that I so desperately want? It's you, Miss Granz. I want you."

"What?!?" Pete, my dad, and I all exclaim in unison.

This is the first time Pete has spoken up since he admitted what he's done.

His mother laughs and sets her tea cup down on the table next to her. "Don't look so surprised, Miss Granz. You know I want you to work for me and the offer still stands. Once I have you sitting in your father's seat as CEO of Granz Textiles, it will be as if nothing ever happened. Well, except that the company will be owned by Ferro Corp. Just be thankful I intercepted the paparazzi before this became headline news."

She reaches back into her briefcase and hands a stack of pictures to my dad. "Just think of the scandal this would have been. Regina Granz seen selling corporate information to Ferro Corp only weeks before the takeover." She's all smiles now.

"What? I never... Dad! Don't believe her! She's lying!"

"Really? Then explain this!" My dad tosses the stack of pictures at me. They hit me and scatter, falling to the floor. When I stoop to pick up the pictures, I see myself with Pete and we're in the middle of what looks like a heated embrace. It was from that first night at Ricky's club when we were dancing. Another picture shows Mrs. Ferro and I sitting at a table, a manila envelope being exchanged from one set of hands to the other. The picture is incriminating, making it look like I've been secretly dealing with the Ferros behind my dad's back. It doesn't matter that it's not what happened.

"Dad, you have to believe me. She tricked me into having lunch with her. She wanted to offer me a job. Those were application forms in the envelope. I turned her down. Why would I do this to you?"

"I don't know, Regina. Why do you do anything? For yourself. With complete disregard for your family." Dad doesn't look at me and when he talks, it's as if he's talking to a stranger. "Is this your way of getting back at me because I didn't let you sit in on those meetings? Is that what this is? Are you really that vindictive that you'd sell out your own flesh and blood? You've betrayed this family one too many times Regina. As of this day you are no longer my daughter. You're dead to me."

My legs give way and I'm lucky to be standing in front of a chair because otherwise my ass would be on the floor. My mom sits there stunned. I take her hand and squeeze it. Thankfully, she doesn't let go. I need her support right now.

Everything is coming apart.

Constance cuts in, "You will do no such thing, Mr. Granz. Not if you want your company to stay somewhat in your family. Disown your daughter and you lose everything." Mrs. Ferro stays cool, calm and collected, almost emotionless. She could be ordering her house staff around or picking her toe nails and it would be just as exciting.

"Now, if you agree to my proposal, Ferro Corp will keep Granz Textiles intact, placing Regina at the head of the company as soon as she finishes her graduate studies. We will make sure Granz Textiles will go down your family line through your daughter's lineage. On our side, we will destroy any evidence linking either Peter or Regina to the warehouse incident, keeping them both clean and out of jail."

Looking her in the eye, I ask, "You haven't told us what you want us to agree to. All of this because you want me as CEO of my family's company? It just doesn't make any sense. And how does that keep the company in my family line if it's owned by Ferro Corp?"

"Regina. In the public eye, you are immaculate, completely unsullied.

Everybody loves you. My son, on the other hand, well, let's just say that he's slowly becoming a social pariah and could use some polishing. He could benefit greatly from associating with someone as pristine as you and with such strength of character, especially now that he's the heir. Thanks to my loving family, the Ferro name is becoming tarnished and I will not have it."

"What are you saying?" I repeat.

With a triumphant smile, Mrs. Ferro drops the bomb. "If you agree, Granz Textiles will return to the Granz family in the form of a wedding gift to your husband, which he will then pass down to your first child."

She wants to give a gift to Anthony? I'm lost. I can't see the two by four coming at my head, but I know it's there. I feel it. Mrs. Ferro stands, and steps closer to Peter. She puts a hand on his arm.

When she turns to look at me, my blood curdles. "Miss Granz, let me be the first to congratulate you on your recent engagement."

"Wait, what?" I stutter, shocked.

Her eyes zone in on the diamond ring on my left hand and, with a wry smile, she adds, "Of course we'll have to replace that bobble with a Ferro wedding ring. It's far too petite to be something a Ferro woman would wear."

Pete's brows are mashed together and he's holding his breath, like he didn't see this part coming either. The man knows better than to interrupt, but not me.

"A Ferro what-now?" I lean in closer, like she's speaking pig-latin and I just can't understand.

"You're engaged to my son," she smirks, "as of right now. He proposed. You said yes. Welcome to the family, dear."

COMING SOON:

COVER REVEAL:

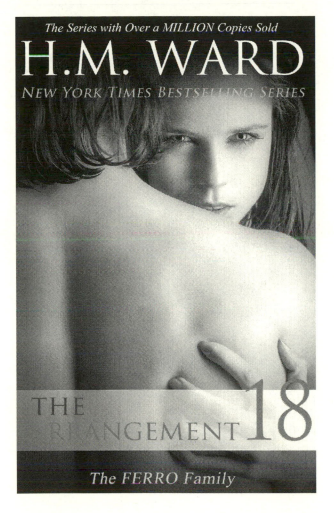

The Series with Over a MILLION Copies Sold

H.M. WARD

NEW YORK TIMES BESTSELLING SERIES

THE
ARRANGEMENT **18**

The FERRO Family

MORE FERRO FAMILY BOOKS

NICK FERRO
~THE WEDDING CONTRACT~
*****

BRYAN FERRO
~THE PROPOSITION~
*****

SEAN FERRO
~THE ARRANGEMENT~
******

PETER FERRO GRANZ
~DAMAGED~
******

JONATHAN FERRO
~STRIPPED~
*****

MORE ROMANCE BY H.M. WARD

SCANDALOUS

SCANDALOUS 2

SECRETS

THE SECRET LIFE OF TRYSTAN SCOTT

DEMON KISSED

CHRISTMAS KISSES

SECOND CHANCES

And more.

To see a full book list, please visit:
www.sexyawesomebooks.com/#!/BOOKS

CAN'T WAIT FOR H.M. WARD'S NEXT STEAMY BOOK?

⭐⭐⭐⭐⭐

Let her know by leaving stars and telling her what you liked about
LIFE BEFORE DAMAGED VOL. 5
in a review!

COVER REVEAL:

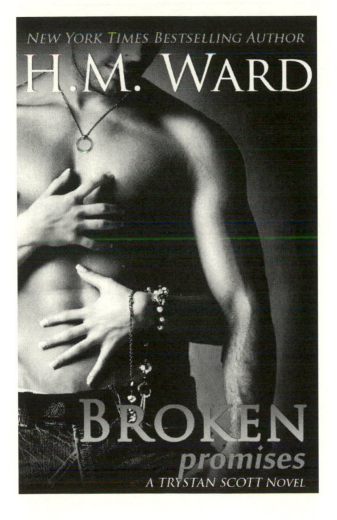

NEW YORK TIMES BESTSELLING AUTHOR

H.M. WARD

BROKEN
promises

A TRYSTAN SCOTT NOVEL